I0694223

Copyright © 2022 Joseph Matick
Published Exclusively and Globally by Far West Press

All rights reserved. No part of this book may be reproduced in any form or by any electronic or mechanical means, including information storage and retrieval systems, without written permission from the publisher or author, except in the case of a reviewer, who may quote brief passages in a review. Scanning, uploading, and electronic distribution of this book or the facilitation of such without the permission of the publisher is prohibited. Your support of the author's rights is appreciated.

This is a work of fiction. All names, characters, businesses, places, events, and incidents are either the products of the author's imagination or used in a fictitious manner. Any resemblance to actual persons, living or dead, or actual events is purely coincidental.

www.farwestpress.com
First Edition
ISBN 979-8-9858067-2-4

"CHERRY WAGON"

OR

MY TAMBOURINE MIND

BY [signature]

<u>*Also by Joseph Matick:*</u>

Animal My Soul *
New American Babble *
Post Meridiem Seasick Fuzz *

Queen Jane Versions ***
Five Times Fast (Jack Jack Jack Jack Jack) ***
Brevity's Rainbow ***
The Ballet (Three scenes from Bedlam, NY) ***
An Official Record of Indiana ***
My Big Blue Son ***

*Available
% The Baba Books (out on Far West Press)

***Unavailable, Out of Print

A Letter

I am burning the candle at both ends. And you are in the center of the wick. A teacher once said, "you will write the next best thing I've ever read." Those who can't do, inspire those who are willing to…to say fuck you to the powers that be. They aren't real. They are not. I am thirty one years old. My name is Jack. This is allegory. My teacher is a prophet. I just got lucky. You will know why soon. It has been three years of quietly fighting for a life. I have been sick to death. I throw up. I get hives and ulcers and still smile and die. I have died. I am still here. You know my name. Say it. Five times. Fast. Jack Jack Jack Jack Jack.

I asked Lydia Lunch for a quote. She asked if I have freckles. Melanoma. I wrote out my cancer. I wrote out my fortune. I cast out the devil with a felt tip pen from Japan. I killed sexual insecurity and Catholic repression and Freudian ideology and academic snobbery and burned down Paris Reviews, New Yorkers and right on time. This novel was due a long time ago. And so was I. My name is Jack. You can use me. I am a literary device. I am all I have sometimes. And if you ever feel like you have nothing, you have Jack.

Yours,

Jack

At Forest Lawn

One / *About Me*

I sit sometimes. Doing this. Which makes so much sense to me. More sense than anything.

Two/ About Forest Lawn

*I*t is where I'm doing the sense making. Cartology. You can see me here now, with many other sense makers. They too, are not dead. They too, do not use the word "cartology." These are just a couple of things we've all got in common. Only— they've learned, through time and how it gets that way— They've learned, how senseless it can be to use words. Yet—

Three / About Them

*T*hey lie peacefully. They don't mind me and how I make so much sense. Right next to them. They're all around. You don't have to go to a cemetery. This is a lawn anyway. It's just like a park. Only we know the names of those buried underneath us. You could imagine how strange a birthday party or kickball, quinceañera would be here. But it happens. All the time. Just at 'parks' where the dead— we pretend are nameless. Nonsense.

Four/Let's Give Them Names

Really good ones. Like Theodora and Appolonia and Iris. And Jack. Jack is a plain name. But a good name. Nobody suspects when you are named Jack — That it is really short for something grand and beautiful. Like the sunset over all of these beautiful bodies — Jackaranda.

My son has asked me this question. He asks me questions like this all of the time. He pretends he doesn't know how nice it is to hear. And how rarely it is asked or how often people answer. The people here at Forest Lawn know. They know to keep quiet about that and all of the other things that we have no business and no ability to explain. Either they really are dead. Or they are really good and respectful. I'd like to believe.

Six/My Shadow

*T*hree things I never leave home without. 1. My camera. 2. My lungs and my pen. 3. My shadow, which sometimes hides and is sometimes elephant sized. And as you can see at Forest Lawn at 5:00 or 5:30 PM — Sometimes, it is so graceful. It grows as the sun sets. Stretching miles and miles until you can't tell where it is. It is not in hiding, though. No. It's everywhere. Like the folks here.

Seven/More on This

*S*ome like to hide from their shadow. That is a nonsense thing we do. But I am very lucky. And you are too, if you are me. People like us, have playful shadows. They may hide, but we know that it's not for long. It's always there. And it's always here. And like clockwork it becomes a part of all you see as me and you. We're a good one.

Eight/Tonight

*T*ogether, we will return home with all of those three things I never leave home without. And we're just going to believe they're all still there. The camera, the pen and thing and the shadow. I think that makes sense. But that may take until daytime for the doubtful.

Nine/For Now

The sun sets over our deadly beloveds. In loving memory they are tucked into our shadows. Those of us outside at least. They don't call themselves dead. And only because they are not. They are also not where you left them. They mingle with the children playing ball. They laugh at the shadows we hide from. It freaks people out when they figure out they're inside all of us. Like our shadows. Who do not know and do not care if we know, acknowledge, or are afraid of them.

Ten/Be Not Afraid

There is a reason they are laughing.

Eleven/Why Do I Know This

I do not know this. But it is useful for you to know why people think they know this. All of us are sometimes very caught up in explanation.

Twelve/I Sometimes Wonder

*D*id they bury me here? It makes sense...I live very close to here. I do what I'm doing here. Which makes more sense than anything. Remember?

Thirteen/Remember

I'm not at the cafe where you left me. Where I handed you this book. I'm in Los Angeles. At Forest Lawn, like I mentioned. With Lily Steele Manley and William Thomas O' Connell and B. Scott Miller and George T. Barrett Jr. They are in the air, they are in the ground. They are all over.

Fourteen/The Two Over My Left

They were married. I do not know this. But— if you take what you're given....Well, they're buried right by each other. Lily Steele Manley left a message. In memory. In quotations. "You are with Us."

Fifteen/"You Never Get Lonely Next to a Tree Out Here"

That is a pricey message to leave behind. The messages aren't too big here. The people don't make a big deal. It's pretty obvious to them. And to you now, when we are me, why.

Sixteen/I Love This Tree Though

And you would too, if you could see it. When will we come here together? The tree makes more sense than anything. You and me and the tree make three. Plus all these other folks.

Seventeen/Why is it Time to Go

We make up reasons for everything. However, I am very excited for the next place. It's got a beautiful name. Just like you. And I'm going to make you a beautiful present. And you'll never have to wonder where I was or why I was. You will just know. Like the party with the laughing shadows of us all. Like the questions that are unnamed and unanswered. Like everyone here. If you are me, you're crying. *Why is it so beautiful.*

Epilogue/Why I Didn't End Things Here

I have an answer for you. It's because it makes more sense than anything. And the tree. The tree is still really nice. And it will be tomorrow.

Jane

One/There is Someone

*T*here always is. There is someone and I'm very close. You and everyone around me knows how close. Because I know how close. And you've understood enough to believe whatever I'm headed toward was worth it. You've understood that we couldn't know what to call this thing. And we understood together not to fucking ruin it by calling it anything too soon. All artists should enjoy themselves. All living creatures are all artists full time. If you clean shit for a living, that's art. Fine art. Only you know the art you want to make. The fireplace is on and someone is close.

Two/Her Name is Jane

*A*nd you want to tell her you love her. But you want to tell her you love me, or "you" for the first time probably ever—at least, this intimately. And you want to tell her she's gotta love herself enough at least, for you to disappear and her to be fine. You don't plan on disappearing, but you've seen crazy shit. For example, she just appeared.

Five/"Hey Joe," Says Jane

I poured us some tea. "Do you like rooibos?" asked Jack. "Milk, honey?" "No milk," said Jane. "Thanks, Honey." Jane is very clever. I try to keep up. "Bitters?" I ask and with bated breath she exhales…laughing and fanning the flame. "Joseph…" "Will you read me your novel?" No. "Will you read me Jack's novel?"
Yes. And we begin. A Jack walks into a flame. The candle is burning at both ends. And we are at the center of the wick. Enter a feeling. Stage right. I love this part.

Red is the color of everything.

At first I thought to make this book brown "because brown is the color of everything put together!" But no, I thought. Red is the color of everything. Itself. And everything put together. And I am red. And you are red. And we were red all over.

We were living in red, we were. With red sheets and red feelings and red hair and veins. In the country of always red skin. And red with fever, we broke hearts. Protecting our own.

I was feeling blue, playing the reds in the red club. Then at night, when the dawn turned the red sky black, it was the color of it all. And you slept in red dreams.

The Queen Calm of Color spread wide just sat there being okay with all the colors in my head.

Even when I couldn't feel much or pretend.

I was Indigo. Always Indigo and my energy was fire turned blue with heat.

I was the deepest of blue. And you never let on to the fact that we knew.

My blood spilled over the ocean and over the coast, cried for my family or at least the feeling of everything. "Come back to me. Come back!" And you could see him and her and me and them. We were all the color of everything.

*A*ll the same color red flying under the red, red and red flag.

*O*ut of Nowhere, Indiana because your mama was born. In Manila. And out of nowhere, had you. And so that's where I'm going tomorrow— And I'm not bringing much. And they call it a red state, which means nothing nowhere because "politics are the soul's retardant."

They say "people from nothing know nowhere." But vice versa they so truly are. And they are the color red.

"Red wanted to keep writing the rest of the novel in his head, but instead thought you would be able to make the connection. You always do," Jack tells Jane.

"You're flying all over the place," she says. I wasn't, but Jack was.

Jack in Flight

*E*very time Jack flew, he wrote. And he wrote. And he would take out his paint pens. The cabin pressure would allow for them to bleed everywhere. And he would bleed color all over his book and write Harmony, his friend. The spilled ink wrote these two poems. They are about her. The one you know, who almost took everything away. And you wonder how he survived. Me too.

I Wonder

If she still sits and marvels, cries
At anything nobly beautiful and exclusive
To, for
Nobody

If she just sits, cries lying
On her back, killing nothing and murders
Me, her
Everyday thinking, thinks
How dare you

If her mother cares about her brutal soul
Or her useless tongue
Long as a bull cock
Limp as Confetti

Anyway, Indiana University is a red and white bannered institution. They call their red, cream and crimson.

The plane begins its descent and overhead
Red hears,

"Hello! My dear red blood world!
My blue sea sky draped world
My fist fighting tearing tumbling ripping storming
world
Hello, my sacred world!
Holy, my profane world
You have come to my doorstep, no
I have built the house, and
How dare you not see me as equal, no!
We came here together sick and black and ill
With infant fury world!
Come into my arms and let's reacquaint
My love, I've loved!

Hello! My dear desperate!
My triumphant brother!
My hands!

Hello!
Let us together make what we both deserve. I see
something marvelous in us,
You clever, clever impassioned love."

All the altitude is going to my head. And so I must
write to Jane.

Jane,

I expect so much of this world. And of course. I'm giving for this, my life. Nothing less than my whole life.

In spades,
Jack

*J*ack scribbles as the passengers shuffle, thinking, "I could not have imagined a world without you. And now we live in worlds greater than our imagination." He never got the chance to write that down before the plane landed. You have now arrived in the heartland. All the women and men clutching rosarys are free to unbuckle their precaution. The temperature is approximately red.

Sunlight on the 27th comes in dancing over countertop and onto the page, marking involuntary shadow puppets. And on the left, too. And over my left shoulder. The kids come through two by two in 4x4 fashion, barreling through your plans or whatever you call those. And kid one of two throws a fit and it startles you. From the other room your mother asks your father what type of rosary to pray. "Are you sure? Don't you want to pray "x," because "y" always makes you sleepy?"

He answers and they're off. And together unbound. And through the walls, we share in the ecstasies of language and love and surrender. I came here for that and for her birthday and for rest. Over here, it's three hours closer to midnight. My mother is infinite.

And I hear her say "confidence" from the other room. And "mercy." And I feel New York beckon me. From the one they're speaking to.

*M*y mother speaks to me in tongues. Some cannot make out the words. But, I know I can this morning.

OH! PRODIGAL GOOD ONE!
YOU ARE HERE AT LAST TO
SEE OUR DYING HOME ALIVE.
COME TELL US OF YOUR LIFE!
BUT FIRST,
YOUR REMEDIES FROM THE CITY!
FATHER IS UNWELL AND SO AM I, THE CROPS,
THE CHILDREN, THE WORLD.
WHAT MEDICINES
HAVE YOU BROUGHT FROM
THE CITY?
HOW DO YOU PERSIST? TELL US!
BUT, FIRST, THE CITY
IS BLIND AND YOUR SISTER IS CRISIS,
ISIS, ISIS!
WEAK ONE GOD IS COMING!
WE ARE SAVED!
BUT UNTIL
DEATH, SPEAK OF HOW TO LIVE!
HOW ARE YOU?
BUT FIRST, YOUR FATHER IS HEARING
VOICES.

She looked at me as if looking into some familiar forgotten face saying, "what are you staring at?"

She did not know that I was in the cafe. And that I'm Staring at the memorial for George Rogers Clark. And while I'm there, some student shouts assignments from behind the cafe going out of business. She's going to start applying for grad school. She doesn't know what she wants to go for and should really figure it out. She resolves with international business. My brother calls me to say "there are people who plan on getting somewhere and you see the shortcut. And you just believe and find a way to do it." That was really nice. The student behind me wants to get married in a castle. She might, I think.

*I*n the Morningtime, you're a farmboy on a farm and the farmer had a job and a past life as a city boy, married a martyr and a saint, and that was your mother and you sing for thee. And in Morningtime on my mother's birthday, it goes "Morning mother! Mother love! Mother dearest! My affection runs deep, will travel through morning — well through all the seasons and songs and wishing wells, etc. etc. And all that...Good Morning Time! You are irrelevant time! At least today! I remember, I am eternal! And yet, I can't find my wallet!" At the cafe, I imagine it will turn up. But to buy time, I order hot water. Squeeze the lemon out of this book.

Tomorrow, I'll be out of this cafe. Leaving home. For a place called home. Jack wrote,

I'm taking off.
Hey God —
I'm moving.

*A*nd up in the sky, we were again. And I sat in the centre seat and not entirely angry about it. And the gentleman to your right is happy he isn't traveling with his parents.

*A*nd I'm happy he isn't traveling with his parents and to my left is a woman reading "Helter Skelter" and a part of me would like to lean over and say "my friend is a Manson girl in that movie," but the last time I mentioned the literary accompaniment of my neighbor, we together went on a Man's Search for Meaning.

$\mathcal{A}$nd freedom child to my right is now humming and it's not entirely clear. I'd like to tell the woman in front of me that she is the most beautiful woman on the plane and in the world and give her a kiss while lighting a 1972 cigarette from Virginia while brandishing a smile and a brandy. Or at least, a cavalier attitude towards the whole tin can.

$\mathcal{A}$nd everybody would cheer for you and throw roses. Red, red rosas.

"$\mathcal{T}$he airplane is one place we collectively take seriously. Hello. I count seventy seven and I'm not sure if you ever hear a single one of those," Jack's mind says, while being.

"Some people are happy. And some people are not. Get close to the former. Everybody is here because they care," said your mother. And you replied, "You must be a queen in a city you don't get to visit that often. And that city is Los Angeles."

Jack,

Don't get me started on the world. For one, the whole damn place seems tone deaf. Though the symphony persists in the face of this…most notes fall flat. Like flaps from the Jack Tree.

With love,
Jane

Jane,
"There is a practical effort, in part—by the world—to
kidnap you. An impractical effort — en masse — by your
soul to welcome you back. Take pride in the impractical
effort.
When disaster strikes, you must first ask yourself—
Whose disaster? Who are the casualties? Is it my own?
Say who?
Inherit yourself again.
For you are the riches that spill forth infinitude.
You are the simplicity of God when you write and write
in earnest.
And you may feel, sometimes…
As invisible as God."

With love,
Jack

Los Angeles

Twenty / Alice

She doesn't live here yet, but it's her home. And it's hot, California hot, "not stale," she says. Some designers have lived here for fourteen years who are now "over LA." And Alice found me a dog and I promised the publisher something and I promised myself something I will simply not let myself ignore. And to your right you will see a thin red line. The song playing is called "Porpoise Song," which I believe means something.

There is a thin red line to the right and you cannot, simply cannot ignore.

Twenty One/Hey Alice!

"RED! RED! RED! THE KING IS RED! THE WIND IS RED HOT, GOD TOO. EVERYTHING IS RED NOW, we red the news today, oh boy…it was red, red and red all over now baby red, papa red and don't preach to red faces — all of them. Red sermons, red robes. Ready for red? HERE IT COMES! RED RED IS THE SEA SKY. THE PURPLE LIGHTER UNDER YOUR BED. IT'S RED. ALL MY BONES, ARE RED. ALL YOUR REACTIONS ARE RED.

CELEBRITIES DON'T MATTER. AND THEY ARE RED. AND SO IS MATTER, SO IS SCIENCE, MATHEMATICS,

APOLOGIES AND ST. AUGUSTINE'S CONFESSIONS."

October is calm. Because we know who we are today," Jack Proclaimed. That's a good way of saying things," Alice remarked. And then Jack started to think about Alice. And not just because she was there.

Twenty Two/Alice

*A*lice thinks that Jack has a good way of saying things. This is not the reason Jack goes to Alice's home. Or the reason for the weather. But it doesn't hurt. Nothing does around Alice. That's why he goes there. But you can't stay not hurting forever. That catches up to you. "I think you are going to be a big, great, word writer…" says Jasmine, I mean Alice. And before she can lay in the knee jerk follow-up, Jack cuts her off. "I'm not going to be anything. And certainly will be unchanged by the accolade parade they give to people after they die."

Alice, I mean Jasmine can you make him a promise?

"Yes," she states plainly.

"Of course."

Remember this spell for me.

"Thanks Jack."

Don't let anyone ever call you a thing. And don't let you call yourself anything for too long either. You are great and I love you Alice. I want you to know that. And I want you to know that all the time.

A Jack walks into the book.

Stage right. Alice begins to sing.

I love this part.

I WILL DIE RICH AND

WITHOUT A TO-DO LIST!

*AND DO NOT WAIT UNTIL I AM DEAD TO
READ ME MY EULOGY.*

Laughing and smiling she says, "you should see me dreaming."

"That's good Alice. Did you just think of that?" asked Jack.

"Yes," she replied, sometimes wondering why we never do much with our ideas. "I think time will reveal what you actually want to do with your ideas. And it shouldn't trouble you too much to think of "what you are. I don't know why. But that just seems like some sort-of trick we were made to believe" said Jack. Did I just read your mind?

"That was so strange," said Alice

"I know," said Jack. His smile grew. And so did his affection for Alice. Though, his coffee was getting cold. And the cafe was getting dark. His smile grew and you could see his teeth. And you knew Alice could see him. It was so pretty, you could cry.

And that together they were dancing around the fire. And you knew this, you did. And you couldn't explain how he was still at the cafe. Like you can't explain all of these things sometimes.

And you were writing. And you were wondering if the cafe stayed open for all of us. Waiting for your friend to get that ride. The ride he never received, and instead wrote you this book.

Jack went to the bank for this idea. And to be paid for it. "The saying is…'You think my wagon is nice? You should see me dreaming!' Jack offers, to the Man. Jack shakes his hand, signifying a deal.

You see these bumper stickers everywhere now.

*E*ven on the backs of airplanes, rocket ships. The man in the moon has one. His other car is a cherry wagon.

Jack thought about his son.

"Up in the clouds or down in my always Indigo blood, my always Indigo soul. And let me tell you kid, if it ever feels like there's an 'x' on your back or a hex on your soul — just take the avenue up town and follow me. There just ain't, there ain't. And papa don't preach green bullshit," Said Jack to the businessman, realizing he was actually speaking to his son. Not the businessman. Jack thinks about his son. And the not so obvious reasons that he hasn't seen him since recently. His eyes roll into the back of the cockpit. And suddenly he's here.

Twenty Three/Appolonia

My sister came to town. Her name is my name, too. But we call her "Apple."

Jack and Apple went to the esoteric library. I read there once at "The Night for Great American Speech." Back when we were still in love. I closed out the whole damn ceremony. And Guy and Lael and Benjamin cried. He read "Notes from a Native Son." And he wept black tears. And they were the color of it all. And the tears were red. And you kept it together because you were in love. I mean, we were in love. All of us. I read A Hopi Elder's prophecy. And closed with the line "we are the one's we've been waiting for." The crowd went wild. I read that line because it was the last line of the prophecy.

You wandered the commons and found the book. The big, bound red one. And in it, all of the answers. Jack discovered all of the secrets of the universe. Well, he came very near and decided, "it's probably best kept a mystery." And Jack realizes, he's still waiting for something. And a ride is as good a thing to wait for as anything. We order coffee, to give us something to hold on to. Anything, while we wait.

Twenty Four/Bang!

The rain comes and we realize what we're waiting for. This whole scene where everyone marvels at the sky like it's never been there. It's amusement. It's amazement and honestly, who is quite sure? Only know, in those moments — we all seem to be. I dance with King Arthur. It was spellbound and we could all feel the changing of the guard. Back in the ozone, one foot in the eternal. Shaking hands with Andromeda, Phaedra, Etc. Al. Storms and how I accept their message. Sometimes Shriek— Etc.

Doomsday, No! No. No no, no...I take part. The conversation. Spoke thus. "Hear me roar child. These are righteous and noble breaths. Dance with me. Laugh with me. Assume your body. We are back."

I heard the white lit night sky mid day silver say this..."

"You Are allowed."

Twenty Five/In the Time When Money Grew on Dreams

Apple and I made a lot of money selling slogans to bumper sticker companies. These were a few of them.

1. *You're a neon sign in hell serving holy water.*
2. *I think it's weird we all aren't all attached by the mouth as Twins.*
3. *Nobody Cries or Dies in my Office and We Are The Mayor*
4. *Better read than dead. Better lived than dead. Better Red than Red, nothing.*
5. *Speak now or not. Eternity has forever made peace with itself.*
6. *Your name is our name, too. And that is red.*
7. *The Portrait of the Artist as a Young Seance of all Himselves and Yours*
8. *A Portal as the Artist of a young Portrait.*
9. *What Happens Next is unexpected.*
10. *You Begin to Get Stranger. And Strangers begin to get you.*

And somebody shook your tree and then the rain came and you would've said "I can't believe this." But of course, this is a time in the year we spoke not, and in belief. We were here.

And now your sister makes you coffee. She is shouting and it sounds like this.

"YOU RETURNED TO LA WITH ADRENALINE POCKETS AND A FIRE REMEMBERED.
EVERYONE WAS DANCING, BIRDS WERE SHOUTING AND ANXIOUS AND ALONE WE FLEW THE NEST."
"IT GREW ON CAPITAL HILL WITH THE MAN IN THE HAT.
WITH THE WAND ATOP SEA
CARVING ON ALL HIS MARBLES, LOSING THEM.
FINDING THEM, DICE IN HAND. OBSERVING PROBABILITY HIS WHOLE LIFE AND OHH HOW THE GODS AND ODDS SPOKE SO EAGERLY IN YOUR FAVOR."
"AND ATOP THE HILL THE MONEY TREES GREW WHILE OLD HATS CHUCKED AND CHOPPED, EXCHANGING CURRENCY TO THE INDUSTRY MAN AT DAWN AND THE FLOWN BIRDS FLEW HIGH AND WITH A DIFFERENT PERSPECTIVE DEEMED IT TRUE
"TREES GROW ON TREES, MONEY GROWS ON MONEY
PLAY ALL OF YOUR MONEY
AND MAKE WORK, WORK FOR YOU" AND THE MAN SAID "YES IT CAN BE VERY EASILY DONE" WITH And With THE CROWN TIRED
THE TOWN CRIER, WEPT SAYING
YES IT CAN BE VERY EASILY DONE
AND IT WAS EASILY ABUNDANT
AS THE TOWN GREW IN POCKETS AND PEACE OF MIND"

Twenty Two/

℘eople found all sorts of ways to make money. Even though it grew on trees. People would walk dogs for money. They would bag groceries.

M AK E THINGS. Especially making things. My friend Penny made money wearing glasses. They would take a photo of the glasses. And the glasses would be on her face. And then her face would get sold to a store owner shop keep and displayed in the window. She passes the frame. People like Penny are in windows and magazines all around the world. People made money making magazines, too. And then, some people just made money to pass time. These were folks who could not make time.

I told Penny, I would have been there, in the same window together. Looking in the same direction. But my head was weird and not around. "The glasses do not fit a head that's not around," I said. "I get it," said Claire. "Maybe someday the right time will come for us."

I do not think she makes time. I did not tell her that even though my head was weird and not around, I was still making money. I was making money, spending time. At the café where I gave you this book.

*I*n America, even now -in the year 1997, It is a strange place where most people watched The Sandlot growing up, if they are your age when you were writing the novel. You know, if you really wanted to hit the consciousness of wandering bookstore souls, you may've titled this book, "Apple Pie from New York During the Seventh Inning of a Baseball Game That was The Ballet in Some Year When People were Only Black and White and Had to Maybe Sit Still for Thirty Seconds While Their Picture was Taken Only to Come Out Looking Like They Were Covered in Tin," you thought. "Everyone's memory has been condensed to some concentrate," Jack says aloud. And standing up, looking at the mirror, he thinks of the words "lemonade" and "concentrate." Milk and Sardines.

I need to fall in love.

That's an American and non- American past-time I could get behind. "You can write the next chapter in your head," Jack thought. And walking out the door, smiling at the neighbors, we left to meet an old friend. To pass the time.

*J*ack Meets An Old Friend and said the following, verbatim.

"HEY FRIEND, who I love and who is an old friend. I can't wait to follow you while I lead in my wagon. Feels like an old cigar. We're gonna have a great time. Sparing to-dos and spare tires and maybe the beach or some green, green grass and the non red plans.

It seems we're meeting as professional children. All rosy red faced n' all. I'd like to tell you how funny it is and humbly admit — I used to feel the need to impress you. What a relief to hear you feel the same. Let's drive away. I'll bring red paint.

In case the ocean wants to show you its true colors.

Red hot my blood, head, forehead mouth, tongue red brain
    Red, because you read my mind and then not enough
    to leave uncertain the big mystery and now i am
    teen heats and young hearts wonder why we discussed everything —
    every avenue down no love land
    Still, let's hold each other — our breathe, saying "goodbye and i hope eternity doesn't pass until i get a swing at seeing us as a pair
    not set in their ways," refusing to.

The sunset was national geographic and you wait patiently as the car turns me out from the inside on. And I get back to my plans and you, yours. And we never made it to the heaven or whatever you call---store, touch. Painting my red words pink and I'm lighting all over, don't know why, pink as a pomegranate.

Being touched, the happy warm blankets, bodies and people that understand and don't, in perfect rhythms. Yoga means union. I know that much. And re: union or knowing — I won't claim to know anything as much as I did that moment. These moments. The ones you cry because they're so pretty and then where?

I hope you stay as long as it feels when the sun hold's it's breathe to go down on you. Still hasn't set and there's crickets chirping, rooting for you to fall in love, die and do it again.

Take pictures for your 99 year old selves and no one."

I'm in my smoking jacket having a house, playing the house with my tambourine mind. I'm getting the whole pie in my hands. Cherries are everywhere.

"Can I tell you I love you?"
"Yes, go ahead."
"I love you."
"I know."

And she said "You'd be surprised at how little you sign your own name. Write signatures to yourself, good big ones."

*H*ello. My Name is _______________________.

New York

"It's the city for the ones that move through windows."

one / Seat 37K UA516

I, Jack, am adjusting my amusement. I realize the sir next to me fingering his screen, the man who insisted on the window seat, though he saw me marveling, filming even before take off. I realize mid-flight that he is not looking out the window. And it seems, there is this imaginary boundary between aisle and window, marked by the armrest. This is entirely disregarded by me as I gaze marvelously across his seat, once mine. I feel for a second I am intruding as our perspectives intersect. But I do not break. And I do not care. And I do forget about this boundary. And then slowly, the man casts his gaze upon the massive quilted blanket below us. And he too marvels. And Jack realizes. The mere act of looking with admiration, turning your gaze towards the world with affection eyes...it changes everything. It may be the only viable measure to be taken to achieve peace world round. I believe this. I do, at least...believe.

Two Statues of Belief

*1. I*t is nice, while in flight. It is nice while in flight to know. It is nice to know that you can stand up at any point and walk to the bathroom. Towards the bathroom, even if the overhead lamp has not made it's indication. It is nice to go. Especially during the times, it is indicated that it is not the best time to go. For you--- it is nice, because you know. It is nice to walk into the rest room and admire the paneling and singular beauty of the cabins facility. You, knowing one---you can take photos of anything, any words that jump out of signage places. I capture the words "open door." I snapped the word "access." I caught my self. The lights will turn off if you unlock the door. Most people do not stay in an unlocked airplane bathroom. But if you know, you stay.

*2. A*nd you stay because when you turn out the lights, unlocking yourself, the door is not to open. You know too--- that if it does, it can be remedied very quickly by saying...literally anything. Why do you stay if you know? You stay because though the lights turn off---some other lights, dim lights turn on. Porch. They are like a porch. Or things of summer. That summer on the porch. These lights, like citronella ---they are so warm. They are so nice. I snap some more photos. I snap my fingers and disappear. And I am through this door. And I reappear where the stewardists take breaks and seats and breathers. They have all of the food in the world. And they will give you anything you ask. It is nice to know that you can literally ask anyone for anything at anytime. In this case, a few more Stroopwaffles because you hate a light head. You tell the stewardess, that you would faint as a kid. And you start to wonder why it is so nice and so similar. These two locations---the nurses office. And the back of the plane, in the company of a stewardess.

*T*hey are incomparable areas of great comfort. They are the nicest places you can go as a fifth grader, or flying in a tin can as a thirty year old. They are the nicest places to go if you forget you can teleport. I snapped my fingers and ended up in seat 37K of Flight UA516. There was a man crying, looking outside at some nice warm quilted blanket.

Jane,

I just landed in New York. New York is sometimes called Newark, NJ. I will call my dad who really wants to know if I survived all the sky miles and nothing. And then I will call my friend Ambrose, whose mother married the sky, on fire. And he has a daughter named Indigo. And I believe I just jumped forward a day and it feels as such. Naturally, I will get Flonase. My nose is high from the altitude and it's plumbing feels like what I hear about New Jersey. I might just sit here, reveling in the measures and lengths necessary to maintain the discussion. The only one either is. It's wonderful to hear the other side laugh back in thunder.

With Liberty,

Jack

Tea Leaves

*"W*hen did you write that?" asked Jane. "It was on August 7th," I replied, glancing quickly at her silver spoon.
I don't remember reading that in the manuscript," she says, circling hot water. "Perhaps you were too busy reading tea leaves." Jane before he continues reading the novel, will you tell him that story? Your story. About how you survived.

"One Time" by Jane Bride

I survived in New York on 11c for 12 days. I was happier than I'd ever been. I hopped every gate, turnstile. I never even knew they would bust you for that. Then my friend told me it was possible," said Jane. "And you believe in your friends," we said. "It happened the next night. Be a good friend to yourself, Jack. And keep the conversation as to what's possible

sacred," said Jane.

"What Happens Next?"

"Well, I wrote you a note and then I wrote my son a note." Read it to me. And then if that don't make me happy, well...I'll still love you." She loves me. Did you hear that? Yes Joseph, I mean Jack. Your face is red.

Jane,

Down at the Lobby, they think I'm real successful. I can tell by the way they look and the way that they smile. And the way they always hand me things and ask me about my very exciting night. Today during my very exciting night, I met Aliexiandriana. She has an issue with numbers. Specifically all of the numbers of vowels in her name. And she's got a thing for order, too. She thinks I'm pretty successful too.

And because of things like friends and happiness. And when I tell her about the really bad stuff she doesn't hear it. Because it's hard to hear. She said that all of my books sold very fast. There is no telling how these things go. I walked her home because people get hurt. And I want to be good and not bad. When we got to her door, the door was grey and plain. So I took out a red pen and painted.

"L. E. T. S.   S. T. A. R. T.   H. E. R. E."

It feels good.

I would like to thank my pain.

My blue blood running dry, my blotched ink and Indigo dye.

My stained hands, the burning bush and you.

Hopeful,
Jack

Blue,

44 RUE DE SAN FRANCAIS!
That's where you are, man! You're in France and you
probably don't exactly love that for now…
But, you don't know what love is
The question nobody really wants
Answered. I AM. SWALLOWED
BY MY PALM. I AM.
SWALLOWED BY MY PALM. NOBODY
AND WANT TO KNOW NOTHINGS.
NOBODY AND WANT TO KNOW NOTHINGS!
I HOPE YOU NEVER LEARN THE RULES.
NO I HOPE YOU LEARN THEM SO WELL YOU
KNOW THAT THEY AREN'T.
THEY ARE NOT. YOU CAN WIN. YOU WILL BE
KING.
I AM SEVERE. SWALLOW.
TONGUES
NOBODY GOT A SATISFIED ONE.
AIN'T NOBODY SWALLOWED
BY THE ANSWERS THEY CAN'T RELIEVE
YOU GET FULL OF
YOURSELF, HAVES, NEED, AM
I'M VOMIT, RED. BEEN DEAD KID.
AIN'T NOTHING MATTER, SORRY—THERE
AIN'T NOTHING BUT COLOR
AND YOU DECIDE
WHAT THE WHEEL MEANS. YOU DECIDE!!
AND YOU DECIDE IT TWICE! DECIDE IT
GOOD! NOTHING MATTER TONGUE SWALLOW
NOBODIES, ALL OVER!
IT IS. WE ARE KING NOW. WE ARE KING.
NOTHING MATTERS AND I WILL LOVE ALL OF
YOU. BEEN MADE.

Red

My Son

*H*e's all there is to me. He makes more sense than me doing this. More sense than the tree I mentioned earlier. He sings Hallelujah in my arms. Can't even worry yet. What a genius.

Jane,

I'm writing to let you know I made it back. And I wanted to thank you for the pictures. Even though I haven't looked at them. And even though when I do, it will be too late. But I wanted to let you know I made it home alright and that there were no mean men who shook me up on the way. Even though I took the ratfest beltway and you advised me not to. You were right and they were all around. Before he came and picked me up. To take me home. To let you know that I made it and that I love all of the pictures that I haven't looked at. It makes me happy just to know you looked at a beautiful thing and thought of me. That's enough sometimes and when you're this close to feeling like dying. I ain't gonna die though.

Because it's just a feeling. And we've all had those.

And I suppose I can see your photos now because that was just a feeling and nothing happened. They will look beautiful. And I will feel like I'm there. But I won't be. I will be here. And I will be smiling alright. People will ask everything of you if that's what you give. Guard this time with your life, it is.

Hopeful,

Jack

Jane,

In San Francisco, some girl was going on about a "subtle or obvious message." And how you just don't know. And that's why I wrote what I wrote. Because now everybody can be happy. Even if they just don't know.

I know that some people want to know. That's their thing. But the happy people almost rarely seem to have that as their thing. So it's for them. And for the other people, too-- when they come around.

I know some people that do know everything. They are not famous. Or my friends. Because they can't talk about anything like us. They already figured out the everything. So now, they don't even make words. At least, not like they used to. But still — they put bleach on their eyelids and wax their mustache and they smile. They do this because they get paid to smile. And they do it even though they know it means nothing. And even though people hate to see their smiles. Because it doesn't look real. And even though if they showed their real faces, and everyone could see their stinky teeth and black gums, it would make everyone happier. I only know one really bad person in the whole wide world. It's a secret Jane.

But all of their teeth — they all fell out. They fell out in a very, very bad dream. And she had that dream every night. And even though she wakes up and knows everything and goes to smile at work, she doesn't do it. I think it's because her dreams came true and now she has no teeth. Because now she only makes the bad faces. And now they call the bad faces, "her new smile." And they call her a pioneer of the new smile. The kids don't like it.

I don't hold it against her. Because she has no dreams. No good dreams. And no different dreams.

But I dream of all the smiles for everyone. Even her. But in my dream —

I give it to someone who knows what a life is.

Someone like you Jane. You made all the dying people from the shipwreck warm. And that is why. And you took me in because I survived. And I didn't even have to ask. You always know. Good night Jane.

Your Friend,

Jack

The Tea Leaves the Reading

"Do you take cream?"

Yes Jane, I do. "Do you remember where I was?" Yes. You were writing about people and wishing you had a better memory. But not wishing that bad. You were speaking great detail the vivid horrors of captivity as a three year old in dreams. You were forgetting about the pain you caused me. There's this though, you remember this. The water was warm. The books sold out and Jack made millions. Everyone was clean and relieved to have survived the war. The one we never signed up for and never believed in. And the mystic whisper interrupts your train of thought. And suddenly, you realize you wrote a prophecy your entire life. Everyone was happy. Everyone had several kids. You made it as a storyteller. All fat and rich, but not fat. You worried very hard and received many rewards for your efforts. We took it all so seriously until there was no more time for that. And in the end we remembered your name and all Gods went to heaven.

"That's good enough to end the chapter. The whole book," she said, and begins making coffee. A constant in any city.

The Jack Leaves the Bind

My eyes roll back into the center of the cockpit again. And suddenly, we're here. In flight...no cafe, no fireplace, no Jane or Jack and color is everywhere. The lights go red inside the Boeing 7777. But, really. And I'm looking around. And it takes an inordinate amount of turbulence, before anyone realizes they indeed are on a vessel flying through space. Together we are unconsciously participating in a relatively wild stunt. I honestly don't know how this will end, but Michael Jordan and Pixar and Oz and praying hands and wandering eyes and conversational stained glass breaks. Phrases are flying through the air like the NASA footage when the chips fly out of the bag and fall where they may. If this goes down, I've got all I need. I gave a lot away. I took a lot from this world. I'm okay. And that makes me want to cry. I do. None of this was wasted. And I got to meet you. If this makes it into your hands, may you never forget that you are here. Do not wait for the flight test. Go ahead and love again and again and again and again.

But who am I to give you advice...just a guy with the holy spirit descended into his corduroys, who knows it. Just like you. If you get this, you have no excuse to ignore the conversation with life. And you don't need one. It gets so hard. Before it gets good. And sometimes, it just ends right then. We love your part.

What to make of all of this I have made?
A totem for a thoughtless, nameless altar boy
reference material for the newly deceased of traditional notions of heart, beating st
yet making sense to no one, but his will.
And will it read my epitaph
how great his sorrows greater his laugh?
And we all cry home.
Not knowing I'm off to build another and lay not dead, but foundation
for something outside all lost sensation
in the land of milk and bitters.
When foreign tongues spoke, loftily to gods and no one, no one could hear
and men would scoff and women, children laugh then lose out on love.
A love so ideal. It was inaccessible, even to him.
And what was he after then? The nothing before.
And in he who saw everything was asked upon more
saying, "now, what do we walk upon? Take to the floor!"
I do, I do! I see, I see!
Alone we can't stand and fall upon knees
to fall upon prayer saying "sanctify me!"
for all the birds who've flown and fall upon leaves.
And wither by winter, back into my roots
wrapped into my limbs I press upon boots.
Let me die, while I'm walking.Let me die in my age.
Let me take my will with me. Let me take to the stage.
Let me crown upon roses. Bloody me with the truth.
I've bled for my head to grow out of it's youth.
I've dreamt of a summer, I laid down in awe
and everyone passing, not seeing what I saw.
They sawed down my tree. They cut out my roots.
And for the first time walked blindly again
I took to the woods with my heart in my hand.

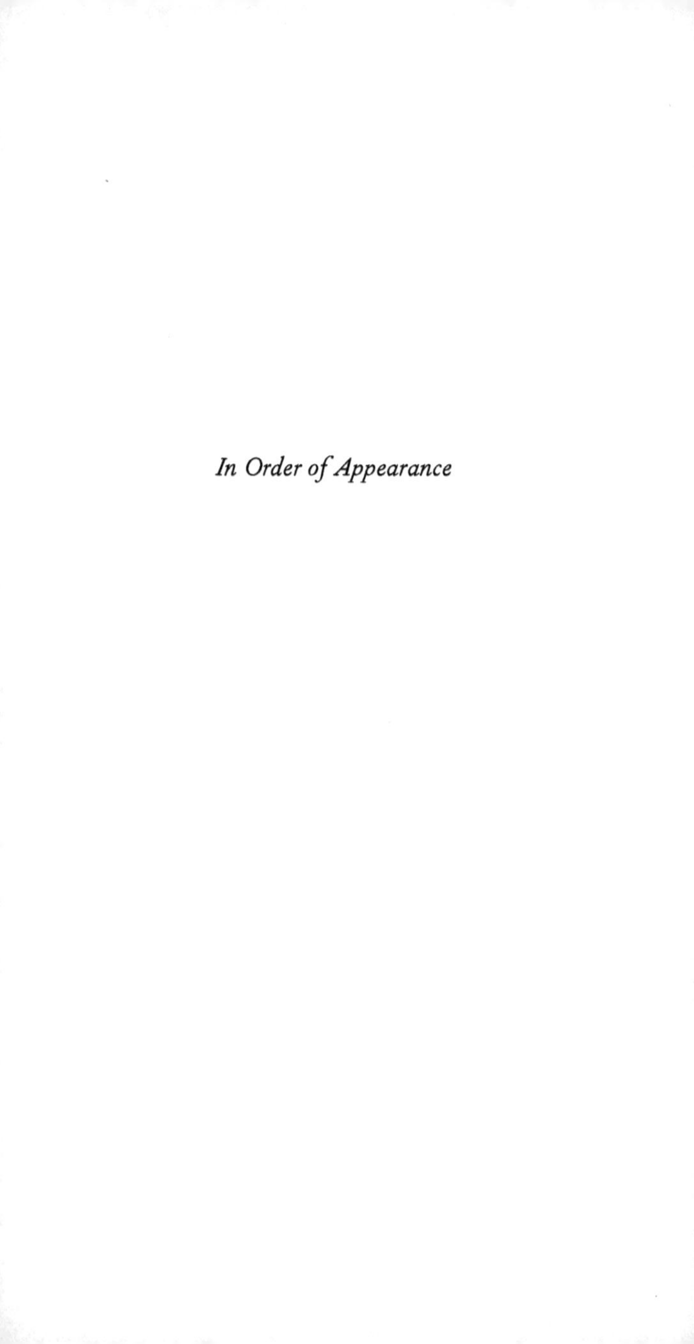

In Order of Appearance

Red in 87´

Jack as "Red" 87'

Harmony at rehearsal, 96´

Hannah, 97´

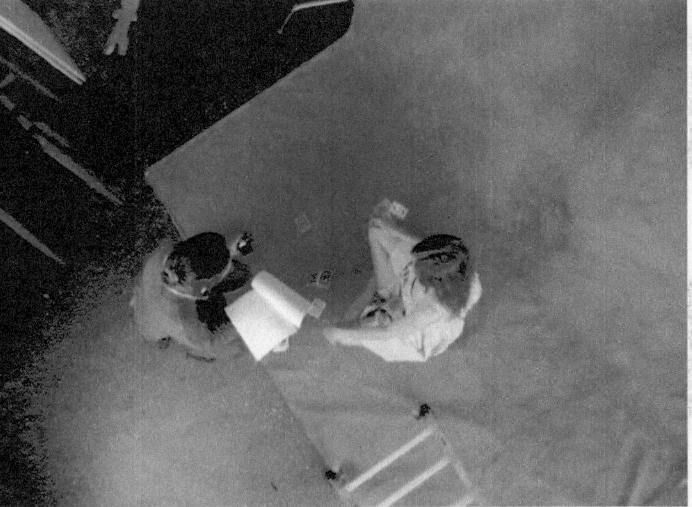

Jack and Jane 97´ (105)

Theodora 88

*A*ttribution

*P*arker Love Bowling, Victoria Cassinova, Talulla Echo Steele (who is also responsible for some very impressive art that will be in the next edition), Hannah Vandermolen, Jaylen and Maddie.

all photographs taken by Colin Jones and Joseph Matick of

Sundaylands.

Also Out On Far West

farwestpress.com

+1 (541)-FAR-WEST

"Completely Original. Brautigan meets Vonne-
gut, meets The Fan Man (a good thing)."
- _Parker Love Bowling_

"I like the way you talk. It seems like you're about
to say something, but would rather keep dancing
around. Trickster, Coyote. Do you have freckles?"
 - _Lydia Lunch_

www.ingramcontent.com/pod-product-compliance
Lightning Source LLC
Chambersburg PA
CBHW020047310726

48970CB00007B/2451